Sally
and
Dave
A Slug Story

Felice Arena

Kane/Miller
BOOK PUBLISHERS

Meet Sally.

She's sensational at sports. She's sleek, slim and simply stunning.

Meet Sally's neighbor, Dave.

He's just a common fat slug.

Sally loves to swish, slam dunk, and sink baskets on Saturdays,

and she's super at shooting soccer goals on Sundays.

Dave loves sleeping sideways in his own slime,

and spending time sucking up salsa sauce he's spilled on his satin shirt.

Sometimes Sally shows how superb she is at synchronized swimming,

while Dave shows how superb he is at synchronized sipping.

When it comes to spectacular snowboard stunts, Sally sizzles,

but when it comes to sidewalk sunbathing in summer, Dave sizzles.

"Why don't you get off your slimy slug bottom and
do something special?" Sally sneered one day.
"But I always thought I was special," sighed Dave.
"And I like sitting on my slimy slug bottom."

"I've never heard anything so silly," snapped Sally.
"It's slobs like you that give slugs like me a bad name."

And Sally swiveled on her skateboard and skated away.

Dave started to sob.

For several sleepless nights, he sulked. He was so sad that
he couldn't even sing Seventies' disco songs in the shower.

Then, while slicing a salami sandwich, he saw Sally skating by.
"She's such a showoff! She said some spiteful words to me.
She should say sorry."
So, Dave slithered next door.

"Sally, I may not be as super and sensational as you, but there's no shame in being a common fat slug. I think an apology from you is necessary," he said softly.

Sally was in the middle of doing sixty-six star jumps when she stopped and spun around.

"Say sorry? Yeah, right!"

Sally showed Dave the door and shoved him into the street.

"Now get lost, you slimy slacker," she snarled.

SUDDENLY...

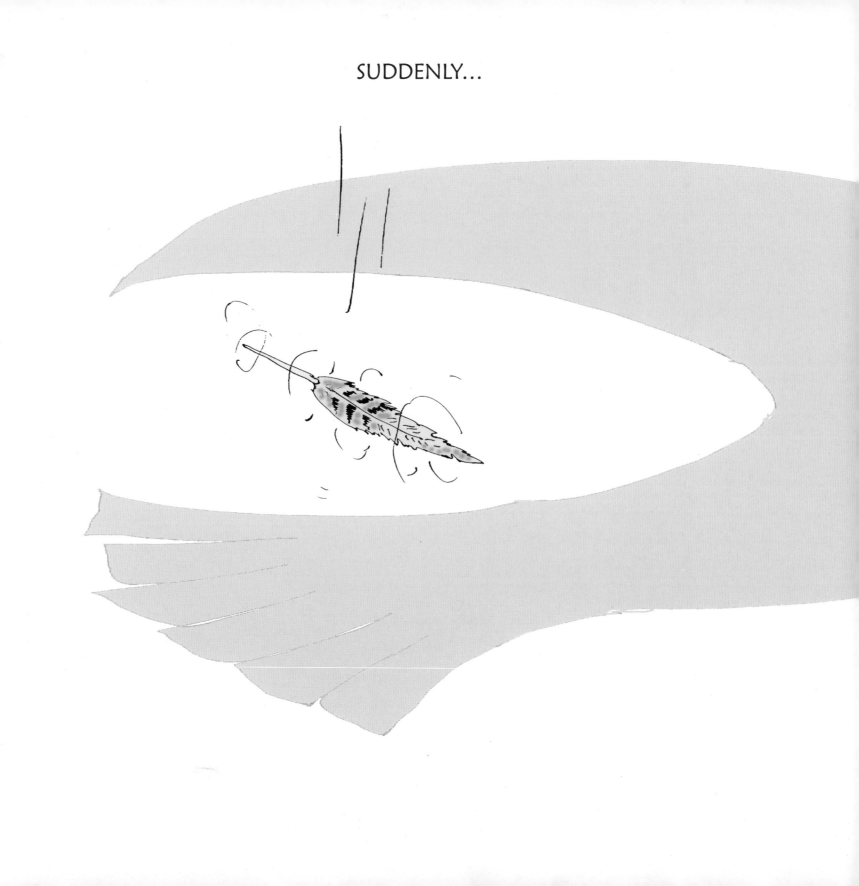

a spooky shadow soared across the slugs.
Sally screamed.

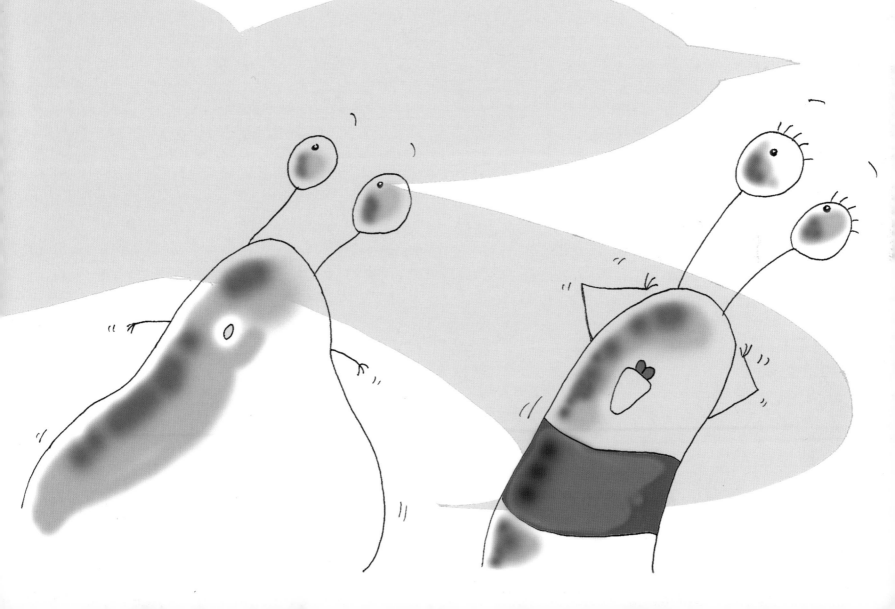

A starving sparrow swooped, and swiftly scooped up Sally.

Sally shrieked as the sparrow shot skywards. "Save me!"
For a split second, Dave smiled, but soon he saw how serious the situation was.

"Hold on, Sally!" he shouted.
Dave sprang from his slimy slug bottom, sucked in some air,
and yelled at the top of his lungs.

"Hey, sparrow! You snatched the wrong slug! How can you savor
something so skinny and scrawny? She's not a meal, not even a snack!
Take me instead – a super-sized scrumptious slug."

The sparrow glanced sideways and swung around.
It shot through the sky, soaring down towards Dave.

"Drop the skinny slug!" Dave shouted.

"No! Stop!" screamed Sally, still squished in the sparrow's beak.

"I'm scared!"

The sparrow released Sally, who spiraled and spun, speeding downwards.

Sally splashed into a sloppy, slushy puddle, which safely broke her fall.

The sparrow continued to spear its way towards Dave.

With only seconds to spare, Dave slid through his slime and into a worm hole...

...slipping to safety just as the sparrow slammed into the side of the street.

Stunned and sore, with a smashed-up beak, the sparrow flew away to the south, never to be seen again.

When Sally felt sure it was safe to surface, she sought Dave out.
"I'm so s-s-s-sorry," she stuttered, still in shock. "Thank you for saving my life."
"And..." said Dave.

"And...you may not be sleek and slim and sensational at sports, but you certainly are special."

And Sally and Dave smiled and slid slowly off into the sunset.

www.felicearena.com

Kane/Miller Book Publishers, Inc.
First American Edition 2008
by Kane/Miller Book Publishers, Inc.
La Jolla, California

Originally published in Australia by the Penguin Group
Penguin Group (Australia) 2007

Library of Congress Control Number: 2007932514
Printed and bound in China
1 2 3 4 5 6 7 8 9 10

ISBN: 978-1-933605-71-5